OLIVER TWIST

CHARLES DICKENS

www.realreads.co.uk

Retold by Gill Tavner
Illustrated by Karen Donnelly

Published by Real Reads Ltd
Stroud, Gloucestershire, UK
www.realreads.co.uk

First published in 2007

ISBN 978-1-906230-00-5

Printed in China by Imago Ltd
Designed by Lucy Guenot
Typeset by Bookcraft Ltd, Stroud, Gloucestershire

CONTENTS

THE CHARACTERS

Oliver Twist

Oliver is an orphan. Is he strong enough to resist Fagin's attempts to make him a thief?

The Artful Dodger

Dodger is Fagin's favourite and very good at his job. Can Oliver trust this new friend?

Fagin

Fagin looks after orphaned boys, as long as they earn him money. Can he make himself rich by turning Oliver into a thief?

Mr Brownlow

Mr Brownlow is a respectable and
warm-hearted old gentleman.
Can his fondness for Oliver
overcome distrust and doubt?

Bill Sikes

Sikes is a hardened criminal who works
with Fagin. Can he control Nancy and
still keep her love? Will he ruin Oliver?

Nancy

Nancy works for Fagin and loves
Bill Sikes; she has a warm heart.
Can she save Oliver?

Mrs Maylie

Mrs Maylie shows Oliver love and
compassion. Is she strong enough
to keep him safe from Fagin?

OLIVER TWIST

Oliver Twist didn't know who had named him.
It wasn't his father, who had never seen him,
and it certainly wasn't his mother, who died
giving birth to him. It was probably someone
in the cold, grey workhouse in which he lived
with hundreds of other orphaned boys.

Life in the workhouse was cruel and hard,
but the worst thing of all was the lack of food. At
meal times, in the cavernous grey stone hall, the
boys queued before the fat Master for their one
ladleful of grey, watery gruel. Having returned
to their hard benches, they would devour their
gruel in seconds, licking their bowls and spoons
so clean that washing up was never necessary.
Still their stomachs rumbled.

They were terribly thin and always hungry.
Not just peckish, really hungry. When they felt
that they could bear it no longer, the orphans
decided to take action. One of them must be

brave enough to ask for more. The boy they chose was Oliver Twist.

The evening arrived. As the boys finished licking their spoons, the room became quiet but for the soft sound of two timid, terrified feet tapping to the front. Oliver looked up at the Master and held out his bowl.

'Please, sir. I want some more.'

Silence.

The Master turned grey and whispered 'More?'

Then he turned from pale grey to crimson.

'MORE?' he bellowed, grabbing Oliver roughly. 'Mr Bumble, come quickly. This boy has asked for MORE!'

Mr Bumble dragged Oliver in front of the owners of the orphanage. They decided that he was a dangerous influence, and they must get rid of him immediately.

So, Oliver was thrown from the only home he remembered and sent to work for a cruel family. The adults worked him hard and beat him, and the children bullied him. Unable to stand it any longer, Oliver ran away.

Oliver could think of only one place to go: London. For seven long and lonely days he trudged along the muddy road. He slept in ditches and had to beg for food. Weak with hunger and misery, and shivering with cold, Oliver eventually reached London, where he sank to the ground. What should he do now? He was completely without friends. Completely without hope.

'Got lodgings? Any food? Any money?' Oliver heard a voice ask.

Fighting back tears, Oliver replied 'No. I have been walking for seven days. I am very tired and hungry.'

The voice introduced itself. 'Dodger. The Artful Dodger's me name.'

Oliver looked up through the blur of his tearful eyes to see a strange sight. The Artful Dodger was about ten years old, small and filthy, with sharp little eyes and a snub nose. He was dressed in a grown man's clothes. A hat struggled to balance right on top of his head.

He half-smiled at Oliver, his hat wobbling.

'Come with me, me old pal,' said the Artful Dodger, holding out his hand and pulling Oliver back onto his blistered feet.

It was very dark when they arrived at their destination. The street was narrow and muddy, and the thick-smelling air was dreadful. Its stench filled Oliver's mouth and nose. Voices of men shouting, children screaming and babies crying filled his ears. Fear filled his thoughts. The Artful Dodger led Oliver up a dark, broken stairway. Oliver held his breath, partly through fear and partly because of the smell.

'Who's this then?'

A shrivelled old face, mean-looking and ugly, peered through the darkness. A cold, bony hand reached out and touched Oliver's face, making him shiver.

'A new pal,' answered The Dodger.

As Oliver's eyes grew used to the candlelight, he saw that the ghastly hand and face belonged to a stooped man with long, matted red hair, a sharp nose and mean, thin lips. Around the room were several rough beds made of old sacks. Four boys, as thin and filthy as the man, were sitting around a table.

'Fagin – this is Oliver Twist,' said The Dodger.

'Glad to see you, young Oliver,' sneered Fagin. 'You'll like it 'ere, won't 'e boys! Ha ha ha.' His laugh sent cold shivers down Oliver's spine.

The boys all laughed too as they crowded around Oliver, searching his pockets for food or money.

Although Oliver suspected that he couldn't trust his new friends, he had no choice. He ate the little food they offered and fell into an exhausted sleep.

Fagin kept Oliver locked in the room for so many days that he became used to the stench and the darkness. He noticed that the boys went out early every morning. They would return late in the evening to give things to Fagin, who then hid the items in a locked chest, cackling and rubbing his hands in delight. 'Good work, me boys, good work.' The boys played games in which they tried to take things from Fagin's pockets without him noticing. One day, Oliver joined in the game. He soon became good at it.

'You're making good progress, young
Oliver,' praised Fagin. 'It's time for The Dodger
to show you how to earn your keep. Watch him
closely and learn well.'

Oliver was delighted at the idea of being
outside again. The next day he cheerfully
followed The Artful Dodger into the street,
wondering where they were going. Suddenly,
The Dodger pushed him into an alley.

'Hush!' he whispered sharply. 'There's our prey.'

Oliver looked and saw a respectable-looking elderly gentleman, smartly dressed in a bottle-green coat, with a bald head and gold-rimmed glasses. He was engrossed in a book at a bookstall, completely unaware of his surroundings, completely unaware of The Artful Dodger who slid up behind him, sly as a fox, and slowly slipped a silk handkerchief from the man's pocket.

With horror and alarm, Oliver's eyes widened.
Time stood still.
Oliver held his breath.

The gentleman noticed that his pocket was empty.

'Stop thief!' he shouted as The Dodger sped away. Confused and frightened, Oliver ran too.

'Stop thief!' more people shouted as they joined in the chase. Everyone was running pell-mell, helter-skelter, slap-dash, tearing through the streets, yelling, swearing. Oliver ran faster, terrified.

'Stop thief!' cried a hundred angry voices.

Oliver was running, panting, stumbling, falling.

Caught.

'You young devil,' roared a red-faced giant of a man, roughly pulling Oliver up by his collar. The blood-thirsty crowd gathered noisily around them like a pack of hungry wolves around a recent kill.

'Wait. Don't hurt him,' cried a lone voice from the back of the pack, just in time.

It was the elderly gentleman. He had finally caught up and could see the terror in the young boy's eyes.

They didn't hurt Oliver, not much anyway. The police arrested him and a few days later Oliver, pale, weak and frightened, found himself in court. Nobody believed that Oliver was innocent except the gentleman who had been robbed, Mr Brownlow. He felt pity for Oliver. He thought he could see something special in Oliver's face. Perhaps he saw his goodness. Perhaps Oliver reminded him of someone he had once loved.

'Poor boy, poor boy,' sighed Mr Brownlow in court. 'I fear that he is ill.' When the court failed to prove that Oliver had stolen the handkerchief, Oliver fainted. Mr Brownlow took him home with him to let him recover.

Back in his dark, dreary, dismal den, Fagin sat at a dirty table, wringing his hands in worry. With him sat a heavily-built brute of a man, Bill Sikes.

'Oliver has been gone for some weeks now,' complained Fagin. 'I'm afraid he may say something that will get us into trouble.'

'Curse the boy,' muttered his companion angrily. After taking a noisy swig of his beer, he looked up with dark, scowling eyes, one of which had been blackened in a fight. He looked dirty and unshaven. 'Curse him!' he thundered, thumping his fist on the table, spilling his beer. 'We must find him.'

Turning to the young lady who stood behind him, he commanded, 'Nancy. You must get the boy back.'

Nancy, who would have been pretty if she had not been so dirty, hungry and tired, looked tenderly at Bill. With a cunning laugh she answered, 'I think I can, Bill dear. I think I can.'

Bill Sikes finished his beer. The three put their heads together and made their plan.

Oliver benefited greatly from the first love and care he remembered receiving in the nine short years of his life. He grew stronger and happier than ever before. He was eager to please Mr Brownlow, who grew to love and trust him in spite of knowing nothing about him.

After some weeks, Mr Brownlow decided to send Oliver on his first errand. Imagine Oliver's pleasure in this proof of Mr Brownlow's trust. Imagine his determination to do the errand well, as he set out in his smart new clothes, carrying books to return to the library and some money to pay a bill. Imagine how proudly Oliver walked.

Now imagine Oliver's confusion when Nancy approached him through the crowd, shouting 'My Brother! Oliver! My dear, sweet, innocent brother!' And imagine his fear and horror when Bill Sikes grabbed him roughly from behind.

'You're coming back to Fagin's with us,' hissed Bill in his ear, holding his arms so tightly that Oliver feared they would break. 'Damn you boy!' cursed Bill, pushing the struggling Oliver through the streets.

Imagine not only Oliver's fear, but also his desperate sadness that he had let Mr Brownlow down.

As the familiar smells of Fagin's room surrounded him, he begged 'Oh please send the books back. Send him back his books and money.'

Bill Sikes spat, laughed, and bolted the door with a bang.

'Be gentle with him, Bill,' Oliver heard Nancy say.

Fagin kept Oliver locked up alone for many days. Oliver wept bitterly to think of Mr Brownlow's disappointment when he realised that Oliver could not be trusted. He wept for the loss of sunlight and for the loss of his one chance of a better life.

'Stop that noise or I'll kill you,' roared Sikes through the door.

'Not unless you kill me first,' argued Nancy bravely. Oliver realised that he had one friend in this terrible place.

Unfortunately, when Fagin beat Oliver his friend was unable to help.

Weeks later, Fagin, Sikes and The Dodger sat huddled around Fagin's table, their heads close together, whispering. Oliver was there too, listening in horror.

'He's the only one small enough to go

through the window,' said Sikes, his dark eyes
fixed on Oliver.

The men were planning a burglary, and
Oliver was to play a part. He trembled with
fear. 'Please don't make me steal,' he pleaded.
They ignored him.

'P–p–p–please don't make me steal,'
begged the terrified Oliver again two nights
later, on a dark, cold night when Sikes pointed
towards a large well-lit house.

'Quiet, vermin,' whispered Sikes. 'You
know your job. Now do it.'

As though dreaming, Oliver crept alone through the dark garden towards the house. Suddenly he heard shouts and voices which seemed to come from everywhere and nowhere. The dream became a nightmare as Oliver heard shots being fired, and he felt a searing pain as a bullet hit him. A cold, deadly feeling crept over his body and he staggered forward, stumbling and tumbling into a ditch. The nightmare ended with the sound of men running away. Then darkness and silence.

Meanwhile, Mr Brownlow had been searching desperately for Oliver. He could not believe that Oliver had betrayed him deliberately, and felt that he must be in trouble. His search led him in unexpected directions as he gradually learned more about Oliver's mysterious past. He was astonished to discover that Oliver was the son of a very dear and very wealthy friend

of his, now dead. Now he knew why Oliver's face had so caught his notice.

Unfortunately, Mr Brownlow's search did not bring him anywhere near to the ditch in which Oliver lay bleeding. His search did not take him to the house where Oliver was carried by a kindly farm worker. Mr Brownlow was a long way away as Oliver began to make a slow but steady recovery, nursed and cared for by a generous Mrs Maylie.

Oliver spent a long and happy time with Mrs Maylie and her niece, growing stronger every day. They cared for him as though he were their own family. Every day, Oliver brought colourful flowers from the hedgerows to decorate the kitchen table. The sweet scent of the flowers always filled the air, competing for attention with the cheerful chirping of the birds as they sang joyfully about a life led in simplicity and goodness.

There was only one cloud in Oliver's blue sky. Somewhere, he feared, Mr Brownlow still felt betrayed, still thought that the kindness he had shown to Oliver had been a great mistake.

Autumn approached, and the first fingers of frost started to sprinkle a whiteness over the morning fields. Flowers became more difficult to find, the birds grew quieter, and Oliver came in from the fields a little earlier every day.

At night, Oliver lay in bed, thinking and reading by candlelight before he blew out the candle and fell contentedly asleep.

What was that?

Oliver sat bolt upright in his bed.

He listened. A slight rustle.

His heart thumped. He stared at the window.

He felt his blood turn cold as he saw the eerie glow of a lantern outside the window. In that glow he saw a face which reminded him of dark, dirty rooms, of grey skies and noisy streets; a face with a sharp nose and mean lips, framed with matted red hair. In less than a second the lantern and the face disappeared, but Oliver was frozen to the spot, wide-eyed and rigid with terror.

Fagin had found him.

Back in London, Fagin and Sikes paced around their cold, dark room. Sikes looked puzzled; Fagin wore an evil grin.

'No Bill, I cannot tell you how I acquired this information. What I can tell you is that

little Oliver is worth money to us now, Bill, he is our little pot of gold.' Fagin rubbed his hands together before continuing, 'His father was a wealthy man. We need to catch Oliver quickly. We need to turn him into one of us: into a liar and a thief. Then his money will be ours.' Fagin's eyes glistened with greed.

Nancy, sitting in the shadows in the corner of the room, pretended to sleep. If anyone had been watching her, they would have seen her skin turn pale, her hands start to tremble, and her breath come in short gasps as she realised that a new danger faced her young friend Oliver.

Nancy had led a bad life, stealing, hurting and lying, but deep down inside she had a good heart. She had only acted badly because she was so poor, and had so little hope in a cruel world. Now she wanted to do some acts of goodness. She wanted to help Oliver.

That night, when Sikes was sound asleep and snoring loudly, Nancy crept nervously out

of the building and walked in a direction that was new to her, through unfamiliar streets. She walked away from the city's squalor towards the freshness of the fields. Hours later, exhausted, she knocked at Mrs Maylie's door.

Nancy's story was long and sad. Mrs Maylie and her niece gasped in horror as she told them how she and Sikes had kidnapped Oliver. But this was nothing compared with the horror they felt when she told them that Fagin and Sikes planned to kidnap Oliver again.

'You must tell us where these men can be found,' urged Mrs Maylie. 'They must be stopped. The police can stop them. Do not return to your old ways. You have shown that you are good at heart. We will help to end your poverty, to change your life into one of goodness.'

Nancy looked sad but determined. 'I have lived with these people all my life. Bad though they may be, I will not betray them. Bad though I may be, I am loyal. I cannot, will not, leave Bill now. He needs me. Your offer is a kind one, but I will not leave Bill. No. You must take Oliver away to safety. I must return to my life.'

'How will we learn more of their plot?' asked Mrs Maylie.

'Every Sunday night, from eleven until the clock strikes twelve, I will walk on London Bridge. You can find me there,' promised Nancy, 'if I am alive.' Her words left a sense of dread in the air as she turned and set off back towards London.

Mrs Maylie and her niece were determined
to keep Oliver safe at any cost. One morning
the three of them were on a visit to London.
Suddenly Oliver turned white, as though he
had seen a ghost. A bald-headed gentleman in a
bottle-green coat and gold-rimmed glasses was
standing reading at a bookstall. Oliver gripped
Mrs Maylie's arm. 'It's him,' he whispered.

'It's Mr Brownlow.'

An hour later, Oliver sat, waiting, in a warm and cosy room. He could hear the mumbling voices of the people most dear to him in the whole world. Mr Brownlow and Mrs Maylie were in the next room, filling in each other's gaps in Oliver's story. They both had a great deal to tell. Mrs Maylie reassured Mr Brownlow that Oliver had never betrayed him.

'He is a child of a noble nature and a warm heart,' she assured him.

'It is as I thought,' smiled Mr Brownlow with relief. He then told her all that he had discovered about Oliver's family. He explained that after Oliver's mother died, his father had married a cruel, heartless woman, with whom he had a son called Monks. Monks and his mother had learned that Oliver was to inherit his dead father's fortune. 'However,' continued Mr Brownlow, 'this fortune can only be his if he has lived without any stain upon his character. If he has ever stolen, his wealth shall pass to Monks.'

Mrs Maylie now understood why Fagin was determined to turn Oliver into a thief, as Nancy had told her. Fagin must know Monks. There was no other explanation. Mrs Maylie shared her suspicions with Mr Brownlow, and told him of Fagin's wicked plot. They agreed that they must go to meet Nancy on London Bridge on Sunday night.

We needn't dwell on the sweet scenes of joy, the tears of gladness and the warmth of

the embraces, when Oliver was brought into
the room. Nor do we need to listen to the
assurances of love and the joyful laughter
which filled Mr Brownlow's house. We shall,
however, note the contrast between this and
the dreadful, bitter, hate-filled atmosphere in
Fagin's room as he began to suspect Nancy's
betrayal. Fagin arranged for one of his boys to
follow her wherever she went.

In the cold, damp darkness below London Bridge, just before the clock struck twelve on Sunday night, Nancy looked at the deadly water of the River Thames and shivered. She frequently glanced nervously over her shoulder as, in whispers, she told Mr Brownlow and Mrs Maylie more details of Fagin's plan to capture Oliver again.

Deep in the shadows, pressed close against the wet wall, a dark figure listened carefully. As the conversation ended, he slid quietly away, running swiftly through the streets ahead of Nancy to tell Fagin and Bill Sikes of her betrayal. When Nancy arrived home, Bill Sikes, the man she loved, was waiting for her. A gun was in his hand.

The end of Nancy's short, sad life was brutal. Sikes showed no mercy to the girl who had turned down the chance of a better life just to stay with him. Even Bill Sikes, hardened by poverty and crime, could not look at her crumpled, bleeding body when he had finished.

Cries of 'Murder!' soon filled the London streets, echoing between the cramped buildings, competing with the howling of dogs and the screaming of babies. Trapped by the angry crowds, Bill headed towards the open window. As the thuds of feet thundered up the rotting stairs, he prepared a rope for his escape. He rushed and cursed. He hurried and fumbled. He made a dreadful mistake. The rope failed him as he stumbled through the window. Still cursing, Bill Sikes fell to his death as the crowd burst through the door.

Oliver, Mr Brownlow and Mrs Maylie did not rejoice over these deaths, which marked the end of two hard, unhappy lives. They did, however, rejoice over Oliver's new-found freedom. Oliver joined Mrs Maylie and her niece in their countryside home, where they shared great happiness. They were soon followed by Mr Brownlow, who wanted to stay close to his new friends and was quite tired of living in the dirt and noise of the city.

Oliver had resisted all attempts to destroy his goodness, and so was able to inherit his father's money. Out of kindness and pity, he allowed his half-brother Monks enough money to live comfortably.

Oliver mourned for his friend Nancy who, unlike him, had not taken the opportunity of a better life when it was offered to her.

This leaves us with only two more tales to finish. The Artful Dodger and Fagin were both arrested for their numerous crimes. Oliver and Mr Brownlow had the unpleasant task of visiting Fagin in prison in order to get from him some stolen documents relating to Oliver's fortune.

Bitter and mean to the very end, Fagin sat in his dark prison cell, his face so distorted and pale, his eyes so bloodshot, that he already looked more dead than alive as he awaited his punishment.

Gladly turning away from the prison and
leaving the past behind them, Oliver and
Mr Brownlow walked hand in hand to their
carriage. At last, they headed out
of London towards the clear,
fresh air of their new home,
and towards the love and
goodness of their dear,
true friends.

TAKING THINGS FURTHER

The real read

This *Real Read* version of *Oliver Twist* is a retelling of Charles Dickens' magnificent work. If you would like to read the full novel in all its original splendour, many complete editions are available, from bargain paperbacks to beautifully bound hardbacks. You may well find a copy in your local charity shop.

Filling in the spaces

The loss of so many of Charles Dickens' original words is a sad but necessary part of the shortening process. We have had to make some difficult decisions, omitting subplots and details, some important, some less so, but all interesting. We have also, at times, taken the liberty of combining two events into one, or of giving a character words or actions that originally belong to another. The points below will fill in some of the gaps, but nothing can beat the original.

- Oliver's half-brother, Monks, is behind Fagin's attempts to corrupt Oliver. Monks and his mother, who was Oliver's stepmother, defrauded Oliver of his father's fortune: Monks' keeping it depends upon Oliver being made dishonest.

- When Oliver was born, his dying mother, Agnes, gave the lady looking after her, called Sally, a gold locket, saying that she hoped that one day Oliver would learn all about his mother. Sally reveals this years later, on her own deathbed. This secret eventually passes to Mr Bumble, and then to Monks, who throws the locket, containing a wedding ring inscribed 'Agnes', into the river.

- As a young man, Mr Brownlow was close friends with Edwin Leeford, Oliver's father, now dead. Mr Brownlow, unaware of her identity, has a picture on his wall of Agnes, Oliver's mother. Oliver feels a strange affinity for this picture, which gives the reader a hint of a connection. Furthermore, Mr Brownlow often thinks he sees something familiar in Oliver's face.

- Mr Brownlow discovers Oliver's true identity, and learns about Monks. He succeeds in gaining a full confession from Monks. At the end of the novel, Monks has to explain everything to Oliver. He eventually squanders the money Oliver gives him.

- The first time Nancy slipped out to go to Mrs Maylie's, she drugged Bill Sikes so that he wouldn't notice her absence.

- Bill Sikes is deceived by Fagin into believing that Nancy's betrayal is absolute. Fagin deliberately fails to tell him that Nancy refused to give information about her friends. Fagin successfully manipulates Bill into killing Nancy. He doesn't shoot her, but beats her to death.

- Bill Sikes escapes, and experiences great suffering, after killing Nancy. Some time passes between her murder and his accidental death by hanging.

Back in time

Victorian England was a period of great transition. Having been an agricultural, rural economy, it was moving swiftly towards industrial nationhood. A 'middle class' was emerging, with considerable economic and political influence.

This swift change left many deprived of their traditional means of living, and dependent upon the state. People left their livelihoods in the countryside to seek their fortune in London, increasing the density of poverty there.

Mistakenly, Victorian culture considered poverty a sign of weakness or laziness. The Poor Laws of 1834 stated that people could only receive assistance from the state if they lived and worked in workhouses. Life in workhouses was deliberately made miserable in an attempt to discourage laziness. Workhouse owners often grew rich by depriving their inmates of any comfort.

Charles Dickens experienced poverty at first hand – his father was imprisoned for debt and the young Charles made to work in a warehouse. These experiences affected him deeply.

In *Oliver Twist*, Dickens exposes the nature and consequences of the poverty of his times and the ineffective, often hypocritical, ways in which society dealt with it.

Finding out more

We recommend the following books and websites to gain a greater understanding of Charles Dickens' and Oliver Twist's England:

Books

- Terry Deary, *Loathsome London* (Horrible Histories), Scholastic, 2005.

- Terry Deary, *Vile Victorians* (Horrible Histories), Scholastic, 1994.

- *Victorian London*, Watling Street Publishing, 2004.

- Ann Kramer, *Victorians* (Eyewitness Guides), Dorling Kindersley, 1998.

- Berlie Doherty, *Street Child*, Collins, 1995.

- Peter Ackroyd, *Dickens*, BBC, 2003.

Websites

- www.victorianweb.org

Scholarly information on all aspects of Victorian life, including literature, history and culture.

- www.bbc.co.uk/history/british/victorians

The BBC's interactive site about Victorian Britain, with a wide range of information and activities for all ages.

- www.dickensmuseum.com

Home of the Dickens Museum in London, with details about exhibits, events and lots of helpful links.

- www.dickensworld.co.uk

Dickens World, based in Chatham in Kent, is a themed visitor complex featuring the life, books and times of Charles Dickens.

- www.charlesdickenspage.com

A labour of love dedicated to Dickens, with information about his life and his novels and many useful links.

- www.workhouses.org.uk

Facts, figures and true stories about England's workhouses.

Food for thought

Here are some things to think about if you are reading *Oliver Twist* alone, or ideas for discussion if you are reading it with friends.

In retelling *Oliver Twist* we have tried to recreate, as accurately as possible, Dickens' original plot and characters. We have also tried to imitate aspects of his style. Remember, however, that this is not the original work; thinking about the points below, therefore, can help you begin to understand Charles Dickens' craft. To move forward from here, turn to the full-length version of *Oliver Twist* and lose yourself in his wonderful storytelling.

Starting points

● Which character interests you the most? Why?

● Do you agree that Oliver is naturally good, or is it only through good fortune that he escapes a life of crime?

- How much sympathy do you feel for Nancy, Bill Sikes or Fagin?

- What do you think about the difference between the lives of the wealthy people and the poor people you meet in this story?

- Do you feel that society fails the poor people in *Oliver Twist*?

Themes

What do you think Charles Dickens is saying about the following themes in the story of Oliver Twist?

- childhood poverty
- poverty and crime
- honesty and deceit
- love
- the power of good to overcome evil
- loyalty
- the city and the countryside

Style

Here's a challenge. Can you find paragraphs which contain the following?

- descriptions of setting and atmosphere

- suspense created by repetition, or short sentences and phrases

- the use of alliteration to enhance description or create rhythm

- the use of imagery to enhance description

Look closely at how these paragraphs are written. What do you notice? Can you write a paragraph in the same style?

Symbols

Writers frequently use symbols in their work to deepen the reader's emotions and understanding, and Charles Dickens is no exception. Think about how the symbols in this list match the action in *Oliver Twist*:

- darkness, shadows, fog and night
- brightness and daytime
- the dirt and smells of the city
- the freshness and cleanliness of the countryside